Published by Scholastic Inc.
90 Old Sherman Turnpike, Danbury, Connecticut 06816.

ISBN 0-7172-6819-5

Designed and produced by Bill SMITH STUDIO.

Printed in the U.S.A.
First printing, May 2004

Just Say Please

A Story About
Being Polite

by **Jacqueline A. Ball**
illustrated by
Duendes del Sur

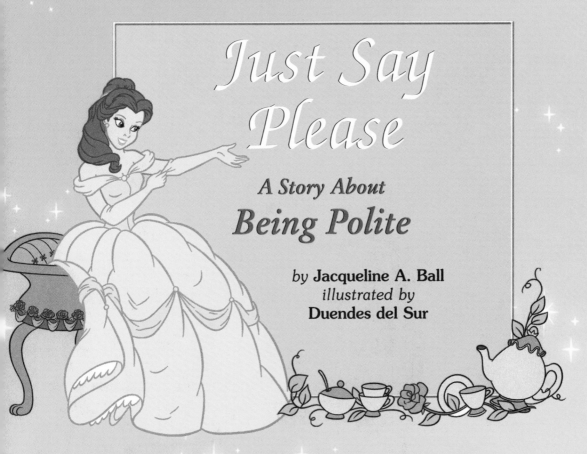

SCHOLASTIC INC.

New York   Toronto   London   Auckland   Sydney
Mexico City   New Delhi   Hong Kong   Buenos Aires

*I*n the Beast's library, Belle and Chip were playing Treasure Hunt. Belle wrote the clues and hid them. Then Chip tried to find them. Each clue led to another, and the last clue led to a treat.

Belle picked up a card. "The first clue says: *Take a look in the big red book.*"

"There's a big red book on the table!" Chip said, jumping up and down.

Drops of water splashed around them. The roof on the Beast's old castle was so full of leaks that it seemed to be raining inside!

Take a look in the big red book!

$\mathcal{B}$elle took a card from the red book. "It says:
Let's have a race to a warm, snug place."

"The fireplace!" cried Chip. "Come on!"

They raced to the fireplace. Chip got there first.
He spotted the edge of a card sticking out from behin
the picture, over the fireplace.

*B*elle removed the card from underneath the picture. "The clue says: *Under the rug is a great big . . .* "

"A great big what, Belle?" asked Chip.

"That's all it says," Belle said. "If you find the last clue, you'll find the answer."

Chip bounced around the room until he found
a card under the rug.

Belle said, "It says: *Hug!* That's your treat!"
She hugged him close.

"Treasure Hunt is lots of fun," Chip said happily.
"You know, if the Beast had more fun, I bet he
wouldn't be so grumpy all the time."

"Why don't you ask him to play sometime?" Belle suggested.

"All right," agreed Chip.

Just then they heard the whistle of a teakettle.

"Mama is making tea," Chip said. "I'll go and see if she's made tea cakes, too!"

Belle settled down to read. Her book had
fallen under the cushion. As she pulled it out,
she felt something else.

*S*he pulled out two keys on a piece of string. "I wonder what these are for," she thought. "I'll ask the Beast later."

She put the keys in her pocket. Wiping drops of water from the arm of her chair, she began to read.

*I*n the kitchen, Mrs. Potts was making cakes
and dodging drips as she talked to Lumiere.

"These leaks are just awful," she said.

"I've been begging the Beast to repair the roof
for weeks," Lumiere told her.

*S*uddenly Chip rushed into the room.

"Mama, Mama!" he called excitedly.

"Hello, dear," Mrs. Potts said. "You know, Chip, it isn't polite to interrupt. And if you simply *must* interrupt, you should say *excuse me.*"

"*Excuse me,*" Chip said. "May I have a tea cake?"

"May I have a tea cake, *what?*" asked Mrs. Potts.

"Um . . . May I have a cake, *please?*"

"Of course, dear," his mother said.

"*Thank you,*" Chip remembered to add.

"Such a polite boy!" said Lumiere.

*J*ust then the Beast burst into the room. He grabbed three cakes without saying *please* or *thank you*.

"I need tools to repair the roof," he said, gobbling the cakes down and scowling up at the leaks. "But I can't find the keys to the toolshed."

"We'll look for them, Master," said Lumiere.
"Will you play Treasure Hunt with Belle and me sometime?" Chip asked the Beast shyly. "It's really fun. Belle invented it."

"I suppose so," the Beast said, taking more cakes. "But not now. I need to find those keys."

Chip brought a cake to Belle. "Thank you, Chip," she said. "That was very thoughtful."

"Belle, is it all right that the Beast isn't polite because he owns the castle?" Chip asked.

"Everyone should be polite," Belle answered. "But it's easy to forget."

Belle and Chip agreed to be extra polite themselves to remind the Beast. Later, while helping h mother serve dinner, Chip said, "Would you like som more potatoes, Belle?"

"Yes, *please. Thank you!*"

"*Excuse me* while I bring in more gravy," said Chi

"*I*'m proud of Chip for being so polite," Belle told the Beast.

But the Beast didn't seem to notice. He kept reaching across the table grabbing for food as drops of water splattered everywhere.

"*T*hese confounded leaks must be fixed!"
the Beast exclaimed. "Cogsworth! Lumiere!"
he called. "I need you in the dining room!"

Cogsworth and Lumiere came running in.
They joined Mrs. Potts and Chip. "Hasn't anyone
seen the keys to the toolshed?" the Beast asked the
group. "Two small keys on a piece of string?"

Everyone except Belle told him they had not
seen the keys.

Quietly reaching inside her pocket, Belle felt the two keys. "They must be the ones he needs," she thought.

Of course, she must return them. But meanwhile, how could she help the Beast remember to be polite?

What would a princess do?

As Belle thought, she reached deeper into her pocket. The cards and pen she had used earlier for clues were still there.

She bent close to Chip and whispered her plan. He grinned and nodded. Then she stood up.

"*Excuse me,*" she said. "But Chip and I want you all to join us in a few minutes for a special treasure hunt in the ballroom."

"Not now!" growled the Beast.

"You said you would sometime," Chip reminded him.

"It will be worth it," Belle assured the Beast. "I promise."

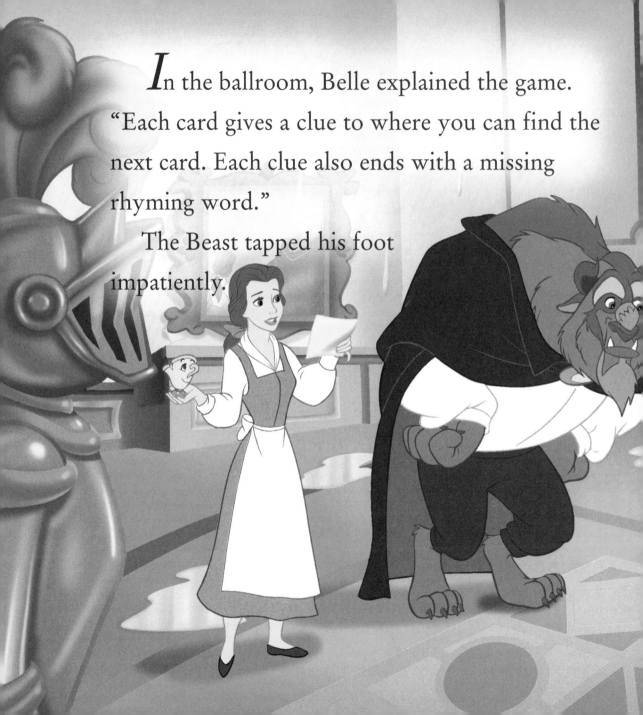

In the ballroom, Belle explained the game. "Each card gives a clue to where you can find the next card. Each clue also ends with a missing rhyming word."

The Beast tapped his foot impatiently.

"*I*'ll read the first one," said Belle, taking a card out of her pocket. "It says: *To see your face is why you use me. To interrupt, you say . . .*"

"*Excuse me!*" called Chip.

"Good, Chip!" exclaimed Mrs. Potts. "And I think the clue is—over there! Behind the mirror!"

Mrs. Potts took down the card and read, *"A knight in armor clanks and clanks. When someone's nice, we should say . . ."*

"Thanks!" Cogsworth and Lumiere called out at the same time.

"This is a waste of time!" growled the Beast. He started to stomp out of the room, but Belle put her hand on his arm.

"Wait one minute," she said. *"Please."*

Cogsworth took a card from the suit of armor by the door. Lumiere read, *"Missing keys are found with ease, if you remember to say . . . "*

*E*veryone's eyes were on the Beast. Now he understood that the treasure hunt was Belle's way of helping him to be polite. He shuffled his feet. Finally, he smiled. *"Please?"* he asked Belle.

$\mathcal{B}$elle smiled back and held out the keys.
The Beast took them and turned to leave the room.
But then he turned back.

"I almost forgot," he said. "*Thank you*, Belle."

"*You're welcome*," she replied happily.

The next day, the Beast repaired the leaky
roof. Cogsworth and Lumiere tried to help him.
All day, the Beast remembered to be polite.
He constantly said *please* and *thank you*.

*B*y late afternoon, all the leaks were repaired.
"What a relief!" sighed Mrs. Potts.

"*Thank you* for mending the roof," Cogsworth said to the Beast.

"*Oui, merci,*" echoed Lumiere.

"*Thank you* all for helping me," the Beast said. He looked at Belle. "Not only with the roof, but with some other important things, too."

The End